I Can't Help a Big Bear!

A BASIC FIRST AID TALE BY NANNY BLU

NANNY BLU
ILLUSRATED BY ANGELA GOOLIAFF

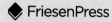 FriesenPress

One Printers Way
Altona, MB R0G 0B0
Canada

www.friesenpress.com

Copyright © 2022 by Nanny Blu
First Edition — 2022

All rights reserved.

Illustrations by Angela Gooliaff.

ISBN
978-1-5255-8995-9 (Hardcover)
978-1-5255-8994-2 (Paperback)
978-1-5255-8996-6 (eBook)

1. JUVENILE FICTION, ANIMALS, BEARS

Distributed to the trade by The Ingram Book Company

Brassy Mouse wants you to come on a short journey with him!

He is going to discover something.
With help from some new friends, he finds out he is
capable of helping someone in need!
He wants you to be with him when he discovers he has hidden
potential and strengths that he didn't believe he had!

To the beautiful children that came in and out of my life during my precious years at Country Fun Family Daycare! These children were a gift to me for the days and years they were with me.

<u>In Surrey, B.C.</u>

Mariah, Amanda, Stefanie, Rachel, David, Michael, Matthew, Brodie, Tara, Samuel, Abby & Kenny, Paul & Lea, Christopher, Garrett, and Danielle & Cambi

<u>In Victoria, B.C.</u>

Nicole & Dillon, Gregory & Melissa, Stephaney, Britney, Michelle, Arek, Jackson, Jean-Robert, Maddi, Zachary, Rebecca, Emili & Nicolas, Ben & Jon, Cadence and Alex

Do you think I could help a big bear?

My brother didn't think so.
But here's what happened, not too long ago...

I'm Brassy Mouse.

My mom gave me that name because of my shiny fur. It really stands out. I live with my mom and dad, and my big brother. Sometimes I'm upset with my family because they think I'm too small to help them do anything. I am pretty small for a mouse, it's true. But I know I can help someone! I always want to help! My mom says that, when I grow up, I will be able to help her in the kitchen. My dad says I'll help him hunt for food when I get bigger. He says I need to be "patient," but I don't remember what that means.

My mom and dad don't tease me, but my big brother does!

He says I'm too furry for a mouse my age, and that my ears are too big. I like to tease him back by using the biggest words I can think of. My dad and I play a game doing that.

My dad tells me that I shouldn't worry, my fur will be shorter and smoother one day, and I'll grow into my ears.

But... all of them agree that I'm good at talking, and talking, and talking...

Maybe that's why they like it when I play outside.

One day, when it was sunny, I took my dark blue backpack and decided to go into the woods. My brother said that I would be too afraid, and that I would come running home. I would show him!

I left a little note for my mom because I didn't want her to worry about me, and I set out on my journey.

So, come on, why don't you follow me?

I started skipping towards the woods, after walking a little way from home. When I turned around, I could see our house in the middle of five other small houses, where some of my friends live. Seeing the lights on inside and smoke coming from the chimney made me happy. I imagined my mom baking cookies, my dad reading a book, and my brother playing with a ball. I could tell they were happy.

I flopped lazily onto a smooth rock. It was just the right size for me. Right next to me was my backpack, stuffed with some snacks and water, in case I got hungry or thirsty.

Please, remind me to pick up my backpack before I go, so I don't forget it in the woods!

I was wearing my favourite vest—the blue vest that my mom had made for me. She said I should wear it when I go on adventures with my brother. I wished we would go on adventures more often. When I thought about my mom, I felt warm inside. She is very special. I was still pretty mad at my brother, so I didn't have warm thoughts about him right then.

After having a little rest and eating a snack,
I was ready to continue my journey.

After an uneventful walk through the woods, I realized I was a long way from home. I sat looking at two different pathways, not knowing which one would lead me back home. I was trying to block out the memory of my mom's stern voice when I go outside to play: **"Don't go too far away from home, Brassy Mouse! The woods are filled with animals that would love to make a tender dinner of a fine little mouse like you."**

I can't be lost, I thought, with a tiny tear rolling down my cheek. "Well... I'm not going to be a scared little mouse!" I declared, sucking in my chest and scampering down the widest path to see where it would lead.

Please, don't let anyone know that I
was just a little bit scared.

As I trudged along, the path became very narrow and steep.
Suddenly, I was tumbling and sliding down the side of a hill, and...

kerplunk, I landed flat on my face.

As I slowly opened my eyes, I saw two big blank eyes
staring back at me. I didn't know what I had landed on.

I was very scared when I realized I had tossed and tumbled

down the hill and landed *smack,* on top of a bear's head!

But it was strange... The bear wasn't moving. Something was very wrong...

This big bear was lying on its side, and it wasn't making any move to catch
me. Was this an animal my mom had told me to watch out for in the
woods? Nervously, I slid down the bear's smooth fur onto the ground.
As I crept away from the bear, I saw something that my uncle Robin had
warned me about, once. It was a leg trap! And it looked like it was
going to eat the big bear's leg.

I saw a lot of blood, and that scared me.

My own little legs started quivering.

What should I do?

I mustered up the courage to speak:

"Are you dead, Big Bear?
Hey, I'm Brassy Mouse! Are you dead?"

I saw Big Bear's eyes open a little and heard him cry.

"Nooo-oh, Brassy Mouse. I'm alive.
Can you please help me?"

"Oh, no, no! I can't help you, Big Bear," I shuddered.

"I'M TOO SMALL TO HELP YOU!"

"My dad says I have to grow up before I can be a good helper. And my brother tells me that I will always be small, and that I'll never grow up."

"I'm sooo thirsty," uttered the injured bear.

I looked around.

"Well, maybe I can get you a little water
from the creek."

I ran off to the edge of the creek that was
meandering along the side of the hill.

I found a broken nutshell and, with all the strength
I could muster, I filled it and carried it back to Big Bear.

It was tough to hold the shell of water and climb up Big Bear's leg.
The shell was only half full of water by the time I got to Big Bear's head.
I had spilled a few drops as I climbed up.

I told Big Bear that he shouldn't drink too much. I remembered that when
my grandpa Tom was hurt, it wasn't good for him to drink water until
the veterinarian could check him to see what was wrong. I remembered
"veterinarian" was the name for an animal doctor. I just tipped enough
water onto Big Bear's lips, so that they weren't so dry.

"Thank you, my friend, thank you for helping me,"
muttered Big Bear.

A minute later, I heard the flapping wings of an eagle overhead.
I slid and hopped off Big Bear again. I ran after the bird, calling out,

"Mr. Eagle, Mr. Eagle, help, help!
I'm Brassy Mouse, and I need someone to help me!"

The eagle heard my scared cry and flew down to see what all the fuss was about.

"How can I help you, Brassy Mouse?"

"I found a big bear caught in a leg trap, and

I'M MUCH TOO SMALL TO HELP!"

"Could you fly to get help?
Remember to come back to the spot where the creek
divides in two, by the huge evergreen tree!"

Mr. Eagle asked if there was any other danger near the bear or me. Without waiting for an answer, he was gone in a flash. As I scampered back to Big Bear, I looked around him to see if anything else might hurt either one of us. There were no other dangers around. I was happy that there wasn't anything else to deal with.

Just then, I heard a swishing sound in the water. I looked down to see a busy-looking beaver with two baby beavers. She was carrying sticks in her mouth and was ready to dive under her fancy house in the creek. "Mrs. Beaver, do you have time to help a friend?" I yelled to get her attention.

Mrs. Beaver stopped in her watery tracks. She dropped the sticks beside her house, turned around quickly, and swam to shore with baby beavers at her side. "How can I help you, my friend?" she asked.

"My name is Brassy Mouse. A big bear is caught in a leg trap,

and I'M MUCH TOO SMALL TO HELP HIM," I cried. "Would you help us, please?"

In a few seconds, the beaver was at my side.
We scuttled back to where Big Bear lay.

With her strong tail, she was able to pry open the trap a little and I managed
to turn the screw holding it together. Luckily it popped the trap open and
we dragged it away from Big Bear's leg.

"I don't know what we can do for him now,"
declared Mrs. Beaver.

Big Bear did look very bad. He was shivering uncontrollably, and he
couldn't keep his eyes open any longer. I didn't want to look at the blood.
I knew that somehow I had to stop the bleeding from his leg and keep
him warm and awake.

"Now... how can we stop the bleeding?"
This would take some thinking...

How about my vest? My mom might be upset with me, but it would make a perfect bandage to stop the bleeding. But first, I remembered my grandpa putting some ointment on a wound to help prevent infection. We didn't have any ointment, though... What could we do?

Can you see anything we could use? Yes, I see it too!

My eyes fell on a pot full of honey. It was Big Bear's honey. It was going to be very useful! I told Mrs. Beaver that my dad had said putting raw honey on a wound could stop dirt from getting into it, and prevent infection.

"How about we use your tail again?" I asked.

"Sure!" she said.

With her huge tail, she slathered honey all over Big Bear's wound. Then, I folded my vest. We wrapped it around the honey-covered wound, and we tied it into a nice tight knot with the tassels to help stop the bleeding. It was not so scary now, with most of the blood covered up, but I didn't like the look of the leg trap on the ground. Mrs. Beaver didn't seem to mind, but it's okay to be scared about some things.

Now we had to think of something to keep Big Bear warm.

I had an idea. I looked at Mrs. Beaver and said,

"Follow me!"

For this, I could use Mrs. Beaver's help again. With her strong teeth, she chomped off giant fern leaves from a nearby bush. Then, we dragged them back and piled them over Big Bear to make a great blanket for him. In a few minutes, he stopped shivering. That was very good.

"It worked!" I exclaimed.

After we finished doing that, I climbed up Big Bear once again.
His eyes were *bearly* open.

"Don't go to sleep, Big Bear," I cried.

"It's not good to go to sleep when you're hurt. Did you know that I went to the hospital once? Me and my best friend were chasing fireflies, and I got caught in some barbed wire. It didn't hurt much, and I didn't even cry. But my mom and dad wanted to make sure that I wouldn't get an infection or anything, so I had to go to the hospital, even though I didn't want to. They wrapped my leg up. I had a bandage on my leg for a while but later I was fine. My mom and dad did the right thing. Tell me about your mom and dad, Big Bear. Tell me about your family. Do you have a brother or a sister? Do you have a grandpa or a grandma? I love my grandpa. He tells me I'm unique. Maybe you are unique too! How come you aren't brown or black, like most bears? Tell me about where you live. If you tell me what your favourite food is, I'll bring you heaps of it when you're all fixed up. We're going to get help for you. We really are, Big Bear!"

"How could he possibly sleep, with you nattering on like you're doing!"
exclaimed Mrs. Beaver.

I was always getting teased about my persistent way of going on about things, but Mrs. Beaver didn't know that this time it was useful. We were so happy when Big Bear opened his eyes!

Me and Mrs. Beaver were exhausted. We both flopped down on Big Bear. But just when we had our first chance to rest, we heard a noisy commotion down the pathway. All of a sudden, there were animals everywhere!

"Mr. Eagle, you came back!" I exclaimed.

"Yes, Brassy Mouse, and we have all the help you will need. Together, we can get Big Bear to a safe place. We found this cart to lay him on, so we can take him to a veterinarian, who will fix him up."

The animals came running to help. Some of them used the leaves that were covering Big Bear to make a bed in the cart. The biggest animals worked together. With their antlers, they used all their strength to lift Big Bear onto the four-wheeled cart. It was big and strong enough to hold Big Bear and some of the animals. Then, we all covered him with more leaves to keep him warm.

Big Bear already looked much better than when I had first seen him.
And who would have thought that he wouldn't try to eat me?

"Brassy Mouse... Come ride with me, please.
We'll drop you off close to your house. It's on our way,"
whispered Big Bear.
"You helped me in many ways, Brassy Mouse. I'm going
to tell everyone how you saved my life today!"

"When you are better,
will you come and meet my family?"
I asked, holding back tears.

"I want to see you again. And my brother will have to
meet you. Otherwise, he won't believe me when I tell him
what happened today!"

When I looked at Big Bear, I could see a smile on his face.
I couldn't wait to tell my mom and dad, and brother, that...
I helped Big Bear today with help from my new friends!
It felt really good!

The cart started moving. I beamed with pride as I nuzzled up between the big furry ears of my newfound friend. I was so grateful for all the animals that helped me help Big Bear. When we reached the path to my house, I gave Big Bear a huge mouse-sized hug. Then, I slid down his soft fur one more time.

As I waved goodbye to my new friends,
I didn't understand why my heart felt like breaking.

**Do you know why I felt sad so
soon after feeling so happy?**

I could see my house in the distance.

I started walking slowly home.

My family must have heard me cry out when I got

close to the house, because they were all at the

open door before I could knock on it.

I had been gone for such a long time!

We sat down on the floor, and I told them everything that had happened. My mom and dad were shocked and proud of what I had done. My brother had a strange look on his face, like he didn't believe me.

A few days later, as I woke up, I remembered
all the new friends I had met. It didn't seem real.
Do you think I dreamed the whole story
in the middle of the night?

I was quite sad again as I dragged myself
out of bed and walked to the kitchen.

Just then, there was a knock at the door. My brother went to open it.

"**What the heck!**" he yelled with surprise.

"A big bear is asking for you, Brassy!"

When I got to the door, I saw all my
new friends standing outside.
I couldn't run fast enough to greet them
and climb up Big Bear once again!
I jumped up into his arm.

With a huge smile I had not seen before, he gave me a very big bear hug.

Turning toward my other new friends, I exclaimed,

"I'm so happy to see all of you! Now I know it wasn't a dream!"

It was true! And now I know...

YOU DON'T HAVE TO BE BIG TO HELP SOMEONE IN NEED!

Please turn the page

for a little quiz about

BRASSY MOUSE and BIG BEAR

FOR THE READER AND LISTENER

In how many ways did Brassy Mouse help to save Big Bear's life?

Brassy Mouse...

1. Brought him a little water. (It is not always a good idea to give an injured person a drink, especially if you don't know what is wrong. If there is no qualified medical attendant to confirm, just wetting the lips can be helpful.)

2. Yelled at the eagle to fly and get help, remembering to tell him to come back to the exact spot where Big Bear was injured. (In real life, you may ask someone to get help and to call 911.)

3. Checked for any more danger near Big Bear or himself. (There could have been another trap nearby, or some broken metal from the trap.)

4. Covered the wound with raw honey. (This can help keep a wound clean and reduce risks of infection.)

5. Used his vest as a bandage on the wound in order to stop the bleeding.

6. Covered Big Bear with fern leaves to keep him warm.

7. Talked to him so he wouldn't fall asleep.

In many incidents relating to injuries, the first person responding to the scene may not have first aid knowledge. This means that they may not be able to provide much medical assistance to the injured person or animal.

*However, the most important thing they need to know is that **many people die from shock before they die of the injury itself.***

No matter what, you can still be instrumental in protecting an injured person's life until medical help arrives. You can send someone to get help, keep the injured person safe from further injury, stop any bleeding, and keep them warm and conscious.

Remember
Even if you think there is nothing you can do to help,
there is always something you can do!

BRASSY MOUSE AND HIS FRIENDS DID!

Brassy Mouse hopes that, while telling this story, he has captured the hearts of children and readers alike.

The examples within this story can help build compassion and self-esteem in children.

Our children and grandchildren will become individuals who will lead, motivate, and help make positive changes in our world!

When a child believes they can do one thing to help someone in need, they can empower themselves by trying. Parents, siblings, grandparents, aunts, uncles, teachers, and friends can help promote this feeling in the child they read to and help with their desire to learn.

Join us in embracing them!
Love their differences!
Encourage them to be the best they can be!

Please help by contacting and encouraging non-profit first aid organizations within Canada, such as St. John's Ambulance and the Canadian Red Cross, to offer workshops/courses for parents and young children between the ages of 4 and 10, in person or online!

Courses for this age group are seldom offered, if at all!

Ask any parent, and they can tell you how smart their 3- or 4-year-old is!
Young children are very capable of learning how to help someone in need.

From each book purchased, you will add to the author's donations, forwarded to organizations such as those mentioned above. The author will also donate to Worldwide humanitarian aid through her Church.

Acknowledgements

To my husband, Bob, family members and friends, who wondered if I would ever get my stories published!

To my oldest son, Sean, who grew up way too fast... but that's another story. To my youngest son, Darren, who ran home from school every day to help me with my daycare children. He was a loving influence to each child that looked up to him.

To my grandchildren...

Lauren, Colin, Keira, Anika, Traver, Jorja, Kael, Naveah, Jacek, Phoenix, Scarlet and Ezra, who continue to amaze me!

To an unexpected new friend, Louise, as she opened her heart to the characters in this story. She helped me edit the story as the characters developed into real friends.

I am very grateful to FriesenPress team members for blessing me with their time and talents, helping me publish my little story.

About the Author

Nanny Blu is thrilled to be publishing her first children's story, almost twenty-four years after writing it.

After operating her own Licensed Family Day Care in Surrey and Victoria, B.C., Canada, she took a writing course, thinking it would be lovely to have her own storybook to read to her grandchildren.

She drew on the experiences of her daycare days, recalling how wonderful it was to encourage children to develop a sense of empowerment and help them believe in themselves.

Part of their playtime was to care for sick teddy bears and dolls. Of course, they had their doctor's kits and nurse's uniforms to help them feel competent in their playtime. But encouraging them to develop a pattern of nurturing after what they read in storybooks or made-up stories was much more of an influence.

Storytime was magical, and finding out what the children could remember of those stories weeks later was remarkable to her.

Her oldest son's ability to read stories in kindergarten, along with receiving an award from the principal, was due to him memorizing the words she read to him, and not to him learning his ABCs.

Publishing her story of Brassy Mouse and his friends became very important to her. It was about wanting to be a part of helping one reader and listener at a time, so they could repeat the process of caring for someone who might need their help one day.

And so it will go on, from one caring person to another.

Nanny Blu thanks you in advance for contacting and encouraging non-profit first aid organizations to add workshops and programs for parents with younger children. This is what she will be supporting herself, in the future.

Printed in Canada